Phnegramises

Eugene Roland Bostwick

For my baby sister Lacey who could say **"Iloveyoutoo"** *while sound asleep.*

Good Morning

The Chasm

I feel alone
Because I have not found you.

Are you the one?

Who will take my hand
and fall with me
through the chasm
toward death

Down

Down

down

In all directions
DOWN
Until all that governs light are our eyes and our souls
Until we are floating above vast and silent graveyards

See the crosses and the statues all have their vigilant
border guards

Eastward Eastward flying until we are placed in this
place

A place beyond reason
A place of this sideways and that
A realm of chaos and multi colored phnegramises

Until we hold each other,
Lose
and most importantly kiss
Oh but then our world becomes brilliant
A rich place of this sideways and that
A realm of beauty

A world that begins in my heart and ends in yours
Our chasm of light, where time has run its course

"Where there is love there is life."
-Mahatma Gandhi

"Being deeply loved by someone gives you strength; loving someone deeply gives you courage."
-Lao-Tzu

"If you judge people, you have no time to love them."
-Mother Theresa

"How shall I hold my soul that it may not be touching yours?"
-Rainer Maria Rilke *Love Song*

If the Sun could See

-for the greatest Muse ever

The brittle and bold dream of life continues
Daring the weak to question all reality
I my love am weak, and for your comfort soothe
Will ride every wave of pale mortality
I do not dislike the sun that rises in the East
And I have tried to see the beauty in the morning star
All of this I fear calls to me but are counted least
Natural wonder pales in comparison to how dear you are
Ah but seeing is not everything, what good are eyes
If seeing means change and trusting your heart
Yet perhaps the heart sees stronger than the eyes
But hasn't the will to compromise or trust a lark

If the sun could see or the morning star hear
They would hold you as close as I want you near

Sand scar

Hold me.
Right here?
Yes.
They sway to every beat.
What once was sour is sweet
Night is day.
Dreams are reality
Reconnection
They stare into each other's eyes and sadness begins to rise.
I have no other heartache than you.
Both close their eyes and engulf each other again
Click
Colors of every shade
Click
Invade
Click
Arouse.

Red boiling in their loins
Purple covering their minds like a blanket
Grey smoothing life from the neck down
Pristine
Reflecting everything
Light and darkness highlighting it all
Everything
From the smallest leaf to the warmest sheets
Plunging and covering
Engulfing
Loving every distant breath
Smelling every atomic wave
Dancing on the taste of forever
Kissing on the wave of never
Never again will they have the opportunity
To show each other how much they love their own self at this moment
Completely opposite
Completely the same
Soul mates of the sand scar game

Shining Sweet Hair

Step with ease sweet shining hair
All you are a part of is there
And when you feel chained and cease to be
Die for a while and be free
Let the waves of unselfish love cover
Hold the hands of home, starlight, friends, and lovers
You are so beautiful where the world does not touch
And while in that garden you have given so much
Now it seems the world around you has changed
No longer in love older feelings older name
Not so and never allow it to be
Love does not die it gets chained and besieged
And over those things which the chains are connected
Are feathers and breath, light as air, perfected
Beautiful, aspiring, wings toward higher realms
Not chained to anything or anyone
Step with ease sweet shining hair
All you are a part of is love and it is there

Aquarius

When I hold you close
I feel grounded and warm
Home is no farther than your eyes
Sanctuary rests upon your scented skin
The morning sun shines proudly upon us and all within
Our Father would bless our union into sacred gardens

Sweet child of the sun
MOTHER of celestial awareness
Wonderful water waving priestess
I want you to trust in sleep
Here on my chest
My embrace will fend off all outside forces
And keep you warm within yourself
Sleep
..............Sleep
.................................Sleep

Your breath is deep

Purring
When I smile it begins to rain
The sun makes every drop animated and alive
Like sleep to the goddess by my side

Ode to Spring

-For Valerie, the tree...

Ode to spring and grass and flowers
Mornings sleeping soundly in the arms of hours
Sunlight creeping over tree and shade
Loving life in the mornings made

Roses to your nose I'll creep
While robins sing songs serenely sweet
Inside your soul my life exists
The flash of your eyes sweet morning bliss
And upon every sacred curve and rise
A vision of heaven before my eyes

Every poem in every book
Every royal gown cross stitched or hooked
Every song ever sung every note ever played
Every lover fallen fast on covered blade
Every painting in every dusty gallery
All pale in comparison to you my love, my Valerie

Within majestic golden moments spent like these
Lives the love of God, a garden, and a tree.

Canopy

Canopy above me
Sure and swift
Your vines contact
me
Making me wish
That I was lost
forever
Smiling
In your circle of
light
Giving up all that is
wrong
For all that is right

Dreams See Now

DREAMS
And eddies of dreams
Each one cascading
Boldly into each other
These mountains take a somber
coloring
In morning
Yet each reflects a perfect dream of
another
SEE
Here at your feet my love
This ocean reaches for you
Needing your presence to make a
dream
Complete
Without your beauty in water
What would an ocean be?
Retract and repeat
NOW
Your beauty, your mind, your eyes
Make these words complete
Devour their shapes and inhale my
dreams each one cascading boldly into
each other

You

-for Marlene

You were the first woman I saw
And understood, beauty.
Glowing
Never letting on what bothered
you
Your belly, a testimony of love
And you radiated that love a
thousand fold
And when at last he was here
You were so tired
I love you because of love
I love you for life
I love you because you are my
friend.

Peppermint Patties, Flowers, and Truth
-for Cathy

You
Have returned me
To the light
Lady fair
And the light
Never seemed so beautiful
As it is
With your presence there
And all my senseless wanderings
Through nights of dark despair
Are gently brushed away
By the tenderness of your beauty
And the fragrance of your hair

All I am
I give to you
There are no words
That can be written
Or any song to sing quite as true
That can measure the breadth and
depth
Of how much
I deeply love you

Daffodil

I have seen the days trickle into nights
And bathed in the nights warm evil delights
And drank in the splendor
And smoked in the splendor
Of clouds looking down on me
Distorting their faces in shame

I have also seen the day relent to the night
Smelled beautiful roses
and children's hair with delight
Looked on love and found it dear
Looked on death and found it clear
I've touched the faces of the future
And kissed the face of the past
A past full of wisdom and light
And the deepness of the daffodil.

Fredericksburg
-for my wife

If my mortal life ended today
And all I am was washed away
At such peace I would be for
loving you
That the very heavens above
Would not know what to do

For a while I walked this
world alone
Quietly seeking solace,
serenity, and home
But never saw I a sky more
blue
Until my eyes feasted quietly
on you
And then it seemed all
searching stopped
... .

My love during these moments
Precious and few
I say the heavens would
Not know what to do
Because I have found paradise
here on earth
Every blessed time that I'm
with you

"But Jesus said, Suffer little children,
and forbid them not, to come unto me:
for of such is the kingdom of heaven"
-Matthew 19:14

"For thy sweet love remembered such
wealth brings
That then I scorn to change my state with
kings"
-Shakespeare Sonnet XXIX

"**I**'ll teach you to ride on the wind's back,
and away we go!"

-Peter Pan, created by J M M Barrie

look here.
Do
You
know me?
a speck of sand
an impulse
staring up
miles
below you

Close to Autism

-For K.K., Jamie, Christian, Philip, Zak, Tyree, and Heather

Around and around we go
Counting all black swans to our hearts

I love you troublemakers
For the joy of the unbalance
The rhyme of the unrhymed
The beauty of spinning forever free
God if only they could see and stop thinking
As IT relates to ME

DO THIS
Walk across the grass where there are walkways
God made green for you
Twinkle wink laugh at the moon
It is yours too

DO NOT FEAR THIS WORLD
They are just different than you

They make order and destroy nature
You make order and incorporate everything
They call out to recognizable fools
You call out to self, pure truth
You see beauty
Where they see boredom
You hear Angels
They hear you
You smell fragrances undreamed of
They smell nothing
You feel the face of God's greatest creation
They simply touch

See this rose?
It is yours
Without thorns
I have cut myself removing them
Gladly

The Beauty of Difference

Send me the ones placed on
the mountains
And all of the ones dropped in
the woods
The ones left behind the
traveling herd
The beautiful ones
Different than society and
culture
Different and beyond the
paltry man made
Realms of earth
Those that defy our
preconceived conventions
The beautiful people put here
to teach the love of God
Daring all to bask
In the beauty of difference

Come
Go with me
I will show you things
Things better left alone but sweet secrets
nonetheless
We'll feast on life's own glow
And deaths pale recompense
We'll challenge the masses
Living forever in each other

Come
Go with me
And Expect EVERYTHING

Blue castles and Dark sunsets
Green roses and red people
Everything you know will look different
And beautiful

Come
Go with me
I love you
And love all we will see

Sandpiper

-for KK my eternal little girl

Running faster than her
little legs
can run
Only to fall into the sandy
arms of the shore and with
Snow white foam emerge
smiling and
Victorious
The sandpipers envy and enjoy
her
As she instinctively runs as
they have always ran.
Yet unlike them she laughs…
Speaks back to the tide…
And in her own beautiful way
Thanks it for existing with
her hands
She knows now that the world
moves
And She
Like the Sandpipers
Laughingly
Moves with it

Energies

-For Jamie, my Arthur

There are great energies moving
All around me
Good, clean, ancient energies
Allowing the trees to talk to the gifted

I have seen it in the smiles on their
faces
And in the sparkle in their eyes
The symmetry of their movements
And their inability to lie

Sometimes they see me as a brother
A playmate and a friend
Sometimes they see me as a hunter
Replacing behaviors with a grin

Sometimes I just stare in awe

There are great energies moving
All around me
Good, clean, ancient energies
Allowing the trees to talk to the gifted

You and I

-For the Queen of the Universe

What a wonder we are
You and I
There are times when nothing else matters
Except you and I
When the shadows of the trees
Bony leafless fingers reaching lightly tickle our faces
Little girl I will try and teach you
But there are some things which only teach
You and I
The way night falls
And summer ends
The way waves crash
And how everything depends
On the way momma smiles upon
You and I
We are more alike than anyone could ever imagine
We see things that others do not
But when it is cold
We shiver
When it is hot
We race
No different than the rest
We hurt, we cry, raw emotions
INTENSIFIED
We love
Very Strongly
And love so much
Those that love us

Listen Loud

Listen loud and you will hear
The sound of hoofs and Brigadiers
Listen loud and you will hear
A waterfall and a castle near

Listen weakly and you will see
The malaise of your mortality
For only when one smiles through life
Listens loud and learns through strife
Can one hear beauty cascading down
And see Angel's deep billowing gowns

TASTE, TOUCH, FEEL, HEAR, and SEE
Louder than our mortality
Breathe deep and walk on stage
Feel every moment loaded and engaged

Listen loud and you will hear
The sound of hoofs and Brigadiers
Listen loud and you will hear
A waterfall and a castle near

Three Angels

We each have a guardian Angel
And children have three
To watch and kiss their brows
And report to the Lord their tenderness
Babies always see them
Floating brilliantly in new world bliss
When little ones reach for them
They quickly teach them to grasp
Then two Angels fly into their hearts
Causing them to glow, smile, and coo
They remain there with pleasure
Until the world is no longer new
Only one stays with them forever

When great balances occur they are near
We call it fate, chance, coincidence, and
luck
The angel beside us
just wants us to see.
We each have a guardian Angel
And children have three

Years Of Chalk

-for Mrs. Grant

In every one of us lives a teacher
But only a few of us have the courage to teach
In every one of us lives a student
Forever changed by the love of a stranger
Now
After years of giving
This is what is left
A quality field of memories made
By every color and every shade
And years of chalk aligned
Across miles of innocent brows
All forever changed and with you now
Years of chalk written during that indescribable moment
When You know You've reached them
Years of chalk across every outfit and hymn
A life walking in the footsteps of the fisherman

And on a familiar shore in some distant year
Where no child has ever known pain or tears
The years of chalk will be counted more
And will be heard on the beach like a mother lion's roar

The Little Girl

-for Maya

"What's going to happen to him momma?"
"He's being punished."
The men with hats throw a rope over a tree.
The women in Sunday dress fan themselves
as if in church.
"Why's he being punished momma?"
"He..he..HE BROKE THE LAW…now
hush child"
The little girl looks at the color of her arms
then up at his curiously
His beaten face is placed in a circle and the
circle hugs his neck.
She looks at her momma who is breathless.
She looks back at the man and he stares into
her soul
Keeping her gaze alone as his neck breaks
The women gasp
The men spit
"What law did he break momma! What
law!"
"He tried to escape child."
She looks at the man again.
Sees the price of freedom
And cries "Why Momma Why?"
Her mother has no answer

“At the touch of love everyone becomes a poet”
-Plato

“He sees Angels in the architecture, spinning in infinity he says hey Hallelujah”
-Paul Simon

“To a wizard there are no coincidences. Every event exists to expose another layer of the soul.”
-Deepak Chopra ***The Way of the Wizard***

The Druid

In a far away land
Among ancient waters and sands
Lives an honorable and friendly druid
His entire life he has spent staring
Into the souls of others
Looking into the eyes of millions
Looking for himself
One day he found himself
In the eyes of a beautiful woman
Who belongs to another

At night he clenches his giant hands
And cries into his bloody palms
Until the pain makes the irony go away
He found himself in the eyes of one
He could never love enough

The Beast

Ripping and tearing he tries destroying
Everything of his former self, shredding all but his
hair
When he drinks he drowns
When he smiles he frowns
When he hurts he cuts to the marrow
Never flinching or pulling away
Except where she is concerned
All the rest especially himself

Are fair game
He no longer clenches his fists
But allows the beast to hurt others
Thriving on cynicism and self loathing
Because of someone he could not love

The child

Finding no solace in knowledge
And no warmth in destroying
The druid casts a spell and becomes a child
With a flash of dust and a few silly words he returns
To a time when love was everywhere
Laughter flowed free and sweet
Clouds were faces and animals
Shadows actually frightened him
The world seemed more alive
And the wise druid liked being there so much
That his entire life became children
For when they saw him they saw one of their own
The druid threw away his robes for patience and reflexes
Loving all children with all his heart
But sometimes
At night
When the druid was alone
After tickling and laughing all day
A tear would roll down his cheek
Splash on his scarred palm
And he would dream of loving her enough that everything became right

Poet, Fool and Clown

-for me

Across a field of emptiness my heart and soul did
leap
Until almost despising and devising went to sleep
My mind awoke so free at last that it could hardly speak
But speak it did and said to me in soft soliloquy

What ails you brother body that all things seem
deprived?
Have not we kissed tried to dismiss and suddenly
come alive
You pent me up inside your skull like a prisoner in
a cage
And only when you're sleeping can I create and
vent my rage
What happened through the years that made you
so afraid?
To create without hesitate as soon as pen was laid
Look inside
Your true mind
A mirror will be found
Search yourself for yourself for the Poet, Fool, and
Clown

So quickly I awoke and then taking pen in hand
I wrote a thousand poems as if on some high
command
My mind was free again, in laughter it bathed and
drowned
Smiling the mirror showed to me
Poet, fool and clown

Monday 11:59 pm

Deep and drowning
Is how Tuesday found him
Before death knocked on the door

Asleep not dreaming
Grown tired of scheming
And watching the moving floor

One hand on the bottle
And his head on in the other
He was glad upon glad for sweet
smothering

Spirited away for a few hours a day
To drunk to cough anymore

Deep and drowning
Is how Tuesday found him
Before death knocked on the door

The Final Hour

The final hour and lords of
power
Casting dice where tombstone
lay
They've made their gamble and
had to scramble
For Shelter with a full days pay
All around is black and brown as
rivers deliver
Dry Sand
We've lived and let live and lost
Gambling on a gambled man

- - -FIRE- - -silence- - -

- - -FIRE- - -silence- - -

Windows implode while
madmen compose
As Rome sits quietly burning
This big blue ball becomes a
star is all
And stops its infernal turning

Light Bringer

What light is this?
That arises out of thin air
What height and breadth?
What sound?
Where only the darkness we bring
exists,
…For but a fleeting moment
And then is gently pushed away
Leaving only a trace of ever being.
What light is this?
That sings everywhere beautifully
Like a chorus of celestial cascading
oceans

Upon this earth today every spring
flower sings
Etching its scent on my soul from the
light which you bring

Flashes

Cars scream by in the dead of
winter
Slow tears down an old black mime
Pictures of youth and summer lie
before me
Visitors of beauty in the dead
seasons rhyme

Perhaps this once while the ice
chills us all
I'll find that place where I was
and stand where I was
For a call
A wish song and a rose sweep madly
over my senses
A baby, a bird, a song of sirens is
heard
While an old man is still outside
mending fences
Blowing the dust off of the
thirteen who looked at the
blackbird

The ice is chiseled from old to new
and will be chiseled again
From me unto you
Ah the blue blaze glows dim when
the air gets thin
But flashes of the past saves the
cold from the wind

“Family is the country of the heart”
-Giuseppe Mazzini

“The happiest moments of my life have been the few which I have passed at home in the bosom of my family.”
-Thomas Jefferson

“I think people that have a brother or sister don't realize how lucky they are. Sure, they fight a lot, but to know that there's always somebody there, somebody that's family.”
-Trey Parker and Matt Stone, South Park

Golden Memories

-for Angel

On this Christmas Morn so fare
I spy my nephew with his mother's
hair
And I reflect back to when children
were we
Freedom and love laced upon golden
memories

Remember rainy days in Ocean City
How we slept in momma's bed
You always wanting the long pillow
While the music of the 70's blared in
our heads

Remember waking up to watch
cartoons
Tiptoeing through the house every
Easter
Water reflecting on the ceiling from
the lagoon
Our eyes were big and our baskets
full and only then would we scream

Remember the Dairy Queen and
grandma's car
Skipper and DeeDee and how cool
they were

Sand-crabs and sandcastles and drinking Yoo-Hoo
Riding waves on Giant rubber rafts that were blue

Remember the hum of long electric heaters
Musty wool blankets, the sound of the wind
And silence
Remember chicken-necking and you screaming
Without sound
The day the crab hung on
Our Dad rushing to you and holding you until the pain
Was gone

My dear sister anytime you have misplaced
Your childhood memories, time, or place
Remember that I was there and for a part of your life
Most of your experiences I shared

This Christmas these rememberances I give to thee
Freedom and love laced upon golden memories

Ma and May

Joy and love and Ma and May
Tumbling through years of sacred days
To arrive awake and aware in a new
place
Where love and peace and touch are
held tight
Tighter
Than the muscles that want war
Tighter
Than the shrouded scepter at the door
A place of complete and utter
peacefulness and view
No two things remembered more
sacred than you
Valleys miles deep with trees of
brilliance hued
Thousands upon thousands of crisp
shining sparkles highlighting each day
Remembering
Dawn
and Joy
and Love
and Ma
and May

Dec 16th

When all the leaves have fallen home
And the holidays are open wide
All of my children are singing of Santa
But in my heart there is a divide
I know that her Christmas
Will be better than any here on earth
But dear God I long to dance with her
And tickle her for all I'm worth
I see her in so many of my children
And thank You for her communicative ways
Her smile gleaming from heaven
On the surface of another child's face

Endure

-for Dan Bragdon

How many have we lost
To the great beyond
So dear and near to us
How many changes must we…
How much loneliness must
we…
How much hurt must we.
ENDURE
How many times will we go
through the motions
We always went though until
we realize that life has
Changed
Our familiar steps are different
because their familiar steps
echo through another hall
Their voices are heard
elsewhere

Remaining in our memories
and souls alone
Not in our ears
Death is the strongest
acknowledgement of how
much we love the ones we love
When we hurt more than any
physical pain endured
We've loved more than we
ever realized we've loved
And that love must continue
and endure
Because it makes us who we
are
And their voices will forever
be heard in our voice
We should not be bitter
because they are gone
They are not
They make us.

"Nature knows no indecencies; man invents them."
-Mark Twain's Notebook

"April is the tuning fork for the summer months ahead."
-Rod McKuen, *April*

"I love to think of nature as an unlimited broadcasting station, through which God speaks to us every hour, if we would only tune in."
-George Washington Carver

A Forest of Trees

-for Lacey

A forest of trees
Gently touching and teasing
Connecting with each other
Through twilight and seasons

All at once
One is beckoned to leave
As all her colors
Fall to the earth and bleed

She is needed to keep others warm
On cold winter nights
They need her fire
So they may bathe in her light

The trees deeply miss her
Their branches hang deep and low
It will be a lonely and bitter winter
Without her hair filling softly with snow

Silt

Calm Thursday morning
More than a little strange
Silence singing in the shadows
Only God knows where it came

Every bird and creeping thing that
moves
Gone
Every Robin, Lark, Duck, Dove and
Crow
To far away for song

Miles away she is turning
Sprung from Caribbean dreams
Of sweat and ice and tempered breath
Listen how the world is silenced while
she sings

She will clear pathways
Where there was land
Inlets where there was sand
Beaches where homes were built
Connecting Mother Ocean to the basal
world of silt

Wind

Feeling the earth move on a cloud covered coast
While the westward wind whispers smoothly of
ghosts
Only the tossing pine trees Answer
Speaking for the living

In early spring they covered us in golden dust
And still late in August keep on giving

There is a Hurricane revolving just off shore
As I sit against furniture piled high in corners
I will await the wind to scream again
And perhaps make a ghost a friend

The Bird

Upon the cusp of sunrise
Where the sand meets the sea
A seagull chuckled "yes, yes" and landed
near the preacher preaching next to me
The message was simply stated
The crowd hung on every word
The man echoed "Is it real?"
And God answered through a bird
Doubtful was I at first, a fancy, a
coincidence
My soul however knows no such difference

Thank you Father for the man's words this
Easter morning
But thank you more Father, for the bird

On the Shore

The water slid
S
I
D
E

W
A
Y
S
Pools developed, put forth and returned
Children were everywhere
One daddy held his one-year-old vision of the world
Every possible footprint was there
Every size, shape, and memory
Washed away slowly, methodically
By the constant reoccurrence
Of the shore

The Shepherd Dreams of Gardens

Under a billowing willow
While sleeping soundly and serene
The shepherd dreams of gardens
And subtle nuances rarely seen
Beauty
Exalted from within
Heroes
Born of sacrifice
Holding babies and fond farewells
Three
Holding hands
Bathed in light
He dreams of all that ever was
And all that ever will be
He sees this shell return to dust
Laughs heartily at the beauty of eternity
And suddenly

SILENCE

All is still
His eyes open and behold a marvelous treat
A bright new star in the quiet evening air
Rising beautifully in the East

Forest Nights

The forest is quiet tonight
Even the brittle leaves
Give little sound
The moon has silenced everything
In its thick glow
Yet beyond the veil of trees I see
Other worlds and other parts of life
Staring back at me
Myriad creatures gaze and twist
Never again alone
As I peer up at an equally questioning
Unknown

Now Night

Night has arrived with her army of
color
Grey lieutenants and purple privates
Colorless corporals and azure
generals
"Command us sweet queen of all
that is sacred"
Sweet night
Sweet delight
Now is the time for our awakening
These hills and mountains, streams,
and meadows
Change when we attack
Let us live in you as you have lived
in us
Altering
Decolorizing
Shifting
Oh sweet saturation
Seeing in…a different view
All things made whole, complete,
renewed
Moonlight far against my face
Thank you thank you thank you
For your eternal and loving embrace

The Sound of Trees

Protectors of the earth
And man and life
Speak to us
Let us hear truth
Catching the wind
The songs of a million maidens
Singing
Shield us from torrents of rain
Through wet nights disarray
Sanctified silence between giant
drops engaged
Speak
Speak
Speak
Through your nests and sways
Of your great comfort and truth
And the power of your shade
Speak

Hello

There, a patch of red
Across the glen
Bursting out of the trees
Crisp clear chilly October morn
The smell of breakfast and sex
A large Sunday paper calling
Right there a patch of red
Across the glen
Waving
Hello
From God

Knave

In an ancient glade
In a classic tyme
Lived a brilliant knave
Who philosophized rhyme

As the rain was falling
And the forest moaned
The hoot owls took shelter
While the knave found a home

Under a canopy of wonder
Against an English oak
The knave brought forth a pen
And from his soul brilliantly wrote

In an ancient glade
In a classic tyme
A brilliant knave
Philosophized rhyme

Oh the moods he felt
Changing space and time
Many animals sat watching
As his pen created rhyme

The sun rose the sun set
Yet he saw no need for rest
When one hand would cramp he would switch
Undying, the first on a quest

The quest to explain in rhyme or none
All the heartaches and joys of life
To put into motion all preconceived notions
And lunge to the heart with his knife

The woods carried him through
As sleep finally came and soothed his weary mind
The birds and woodland creatures tucked him in
Each kissing the brow of the first poet to philosophize rhyme

Radon
-For Sylvia and Deepak

Radon, the upper echelon
The truth to all questions
Moving faster than eons
Laughing in morning and crying at spring
Spring is the thing

Rebirth and renewal

Cycles of existence

Birth -----→
Life ----→

The ups are summer
The downs are fall

Winters leaves whither and die from the vine
Descend into the ground
Nourish the tree
Become part of the tree eventually
Ascend slowly
Until…
….
….
REBIRTH
RENEWAL
Born again

Birth ---→
Life ---→

The ups are summer
The downs are fall

Radon
The upper echelon
The truth to all questions
Moving faster that eons
Laughing in morning and crying at spring

www.ingramcontent.com/pod-product-compliance
Ingram Content Group UK Ltd.
Pitfield, Milton Keynes, MK11 3LW, UK
UKHW041838200726
13854UKWH00003BA/1203

9 781411 60936